LAURA BUSH and JENNA BUSH

Read All About It!

Illustrated by **DENISE BRUNKUS**

HarperCollins*Publishers*

Dedicated to G.W.B. and B.P.B.,
whose love and humor brighten our lives, and to
Tyrones everywhere and the teachers who inspire them
—L.W.B. and J.W.B.

For the love and wisdom of my best teachers—
Mom, Dad, Richard, Dennis, and Karen
—D.B.

Read All About It!
Text copyright © 2008 by Laura Bush and Jenna Bush
Illustrations copyright © 2008 by Denise Brunkus

Library of Congress Cataloging-in-Publication Data is available.
ISBN 978-0-06-156075-0 (trade bdg.) — ISBN 978-0-06- 156076-7 (lib. bdg.)
Typography by Martha Rago
1 2 3 4 5 6 7 8 9 10
❖
First Edition

I'm Tyrone Brown and I rule the school.
I'm a professional student and class clown.

Let me introduce you to my pals. The kid genius in the glasses is Edmund. Jane is the girl with legs like branches. And this is my best friend, Big D.

We always keep our class in line.

And that's Miss Libro, our homeroom teacher. She's *all right*, but we don't exactly see eye to eye.

I told her books are **SO** last year.

It's not that I despise books; I just don't **prefer** them. I like playing freeze tag with my friends and catch with my dad and helping my mom pull the pesky weeds from the front yard. These things are **real.**

As I told you earlier, I rule the school. I love watching Mr. Lumsquitz scratch his head in awe when I solve the math problem of the day, **every day.**

Ms. Toadskin thinks she can gross us out with her science experiments. But I live for that stuff!

*Don't try this at your school.

And of course, I'm the king of the monkey bars. I am everywhere.
Well, everywhere except one place . . .

Miss Libro always says,

"Tyrone, the library is a wonderful place! You never know who you're going to meet in a good book."

I say, "The library is a boring place! All I will meet there are stinky pages."

Every day after lunch,
Miss Libro reads to us.
I sit in the back and use
this time more wisely.

But one day *everything* changed. . . .

Miss Libro was reading a book about an astronaut, which gave me the idea to create a spaceship that I sent orbiting into the chalkboard.

* Pluto, formerly known as a planet.

"TYRONE, please. Save the spaceship for science class and listen! Everyone loves this book," said Miss Libro.

I looked around the classroom. Miss Libro was right. No one—not even Jane—had witnessed the launch of *Spacecraft Tyrone.*

So I listened. And the strangest thing happened: I actually *liked* story hour. And then my whole world turned **upside down.** . . .

On Halloween, Miss Libro was reading us a spooky tale about a ghost named Jasper, when Jasper—a real ghost—appeared and said,

Characters started appearing regularly.

During a story about our Founding Fathers, Benjamin Franklin stepped into our classroom, flying a kite.

On Valentine's Day, Miss Libro read us a fairy tale. Just as the prince was

about to save the princess, a fire-breathing dragon flew in the window.

In the spring, Miss Libro began reading from a chapter book about a pig. She had barely finished the first page when a pudgy pig sat down next to me on the reading carpet.

Read All About It!
BOOK LIST

* If You Give a Pig
   a Pancake
* Olivia
* Charlotte's Web

RULES

Respect Yourself,
Respect Others.

Always Raise
Your Hand.

Follow All
Directions.

No paper airplanes.

Sharpen All Pencils
Before Class.

Fly Kites on
Playground Only.

No fire allowed!

At first we did not want him in our classroom.
He was dirty and disorganized. He ate the most grotesque combination of leftover school lunches.

But as the weeks went by, we fell in love with that butterball. He was witty and kind.

Jane taught him manners, and he began to eat like a proper gentleman. And he took over my role as class clown. His jokes were hilarious.

What does a family of pigs do at an all-you-can-eat buffet?*

And then

a terrible thing happened—
a real crime . . .

*Pig out!

It was a rainy Monday when Miss Libro finished the chapter book.
As she closed the book for the final time, the pig disappeared and
didn't
come
back.

The whole class was in hysterics. We loved our little porker!

When recess came,
I knew what had to be done.

"Don't worry. This pig-napping is just the case for Tyrone and his posse," I said. "Big D, Edmund, Jane, let's go. We'll solve this case if it's the last thing we ever do!"

Jane thought he was in the cafeteria.
"Hurry! Ms. Gravy will cook **anything** she can get her hands on!"

But luckily for the pig, we were having spaghetti for lunch.

Edmund thought he had a lead. "Those oinks coming from Ms. Tonedeaf's room *must* be our pig."

But no . . . it was just the kindergarten class singing
"Old MacDonald Had a Farm."

We were about to give up hope when Big D had a breakthrough in the case.

"I've got it! I bet Coach Smith has recruited him for the football team. He would be great at defense!"

But again there were no leads. Coach Smith said he hadn't seen a pig anywhere.

Recess was almost over, and there was still no sign of our pig.

"Miss Libro, we've searched for our pig *everywhere*, and we still haven't solved the case."

"Are you sure you've looked EVERYWHERE?"

Everywhere. That was it! Of course, we hadn't been *everywhere*. There was one place we hadn't looked. I grabbed my friends, and we were off to save our pig!

they all were! Benjamin Franklin, Jasper the ghost, the dragon, and in the middle of the room . . .

Time to Read!

READ

LIBRARY

library

BOOK DROP

was our pig!

And then I had the most **brilliant** idea *EVER.*
"Miss Libro, let's read *here*, in the library!"

"Take it from me, Tyrone! You never know who you are going to meet when you look in a book!"